The Boxcar Children® Mysteries

THE MYSTERY OF THE SECRET MESSAGE

created by
GERTRUDE CHANDLER WARNER

Illustrated by Charles Tang

ALBERT WHITMAN & Company
Morton Grove, Illinois

Library of Congress Cataloging-in-Publication Data
is available from the Library of Congress

ISBN 0-8075-5429-4 (hardcover)
ISBN 0-8075-5430-8 (paperback)

Cover art by David Cunningham.

Contents

CHAPTER 1

The Mysterious Photograph

"Apple or pumpkin?" Jessie Alden asked her little brother as they sat in Cooke's Drugstore reading the menu.

Six-year-old Benny squeezed his eyes shut. It was hard to choose. He liked both kinds of pie. In fact, he liked *all* kinds of pie!

"Mrs. McGregor made us a pumpkin pie last week," he said, opening his eyes. "So . . . apple!"

"Good choice, Benny," agreed Grandfather Alden. "I'll also have apple pie."

"Me, too," echoed ten-year-old Violet in her soft voice.

"I'll have the same," Jessie said briskly. An orderly twelve-year-old, she rarely had trouble making up her mind. "What about you, Henry?"

At fourteen, Henry was the oldest of the Alden children. When their parents died years ago, Henry helped care for his younger brother and sisters.

Now Henry studied the other items on the menu. Then he closed the plastic-covered folder and announced, "I'm having something different."

Benny stared at his older brother. It wasn't like Henry to order something different from the rest of the Aldens.

"What are you getting?" he asked.

"Apple pie with *ice cream*!" Henry laughed at the surprise on Benny's face.

Mrs. Turner bustled over to clear away their lunch dishes. "Has anybody left room for dessert?" she asked with a knowing wink.

"Five apple pies," said Grandfather Alden.

"One with a big scoop of vanilla ice cream, if it's not too much trouble."

"It's always a pleasure to wait on the Aldens," the waitress said with a hearty laugh.

"And it's always a pleasure to come here," Grandfather said, smiling.

Cooke's Drugstore was one of Greenfield's oldest establishments. The Aldens often stopped in for ice cream sundaes and little things like suntan lotion.

On one side of the store was a long lunch counter with red leather stools. The pharmacy counter stood opposite. A big plate glass window looked out on the town square.

"You know," said Jessie, "this place reminds me of our boxcar."

"It does!" said Violet. "It's long like our boxcar."

"Only our boxcar doesn't have seats that move," said Benny, spinning his stool. "Or a milk shake machine."

Henry laughed. "It's a good thing! You'd be fixing milk shakes anytime you wanted one!"

"I could make milk shakes and sell them from our boxcar," Benny said. "The boxcar could be my drugstore."

"The boxcar can be anything we want it to be," Violet said.

The Alden children spoke fondly of their old home. After they were orphaned, they moved into an abandoned railroad car. When their grandfather found them, he brought the children and their boxcar to his big Connecticut home.

The boxcar held a place of honor in the backyard. The children played in it when they weren't off on another exciting adventure with their grandfather.

Mrs. Turner set a tray of apple pies on the counter. "Sorry this took so long," she said. "But I had to sign for a parcel." She lowered her voice. "I'll sure be glad when Mr. Cooke gets back. That substitute knows about medicine, but he doesn't know much about running this drugstore."

Jessie watched the substitute druggist measure pills into a bottle. Mr. Kirby was a young man with black, bushy hair and thick eyebrows. His hand shook as he poured, causing the pills to rattle.

"He's awfully nervous," Henry observed. "I wonder why."

"You should see the back room," said Mrs. Turner. "Looks like a cyclone hit it. Cartons and mail everyplace. Mr. Cooke will have a fit when he sees the mess."

Grandfather held out his coffee cup for a refill. "I hope John comes back soon from visiting his mother. The Winter Festival is Saturday. Only five days away."

The waitress shook her head. "I don't expect Mr. Cooke back anytime soon. His mother is better, but she's still in the hospital."

James Alden sighed. "We need every member of the town council. There's a lot of work to do."

"We'll help," Benny volunteered.

"I'll take you up on that offer," Grandfather said, smiling. "In fact, we'll start tomorrow. The four of you could clean the Minuteman statue."

"Okay. The Winter Festival sounds like

fun," Violet said. "I hope everybody comes."

"That reminds me," Mrs. Turner said. "Your poster isn't up." She called across the room, "Mr. Kirby, did you put up the festival poster?"

The druggist frowned, drawing his bushy brows together. "Mrs. Turner, I have better things to do than hang posters."

"But the festival is important!" Benny said.

James Alden added, "We're trying to raise money to make repairs in the town square. It's a worthy cause."

Henry spotted a corner of orange cardboard beneath a pile of advertising circulars. "Here's the poster," he declared. "If you give me some tape, I'll hang it."

The waitress handed him a roll of tape. "Put it on the door. That way everybody will see it."

"I'll help you, Henry." Violet slid off her stool and held the poster against the door. Henry secured the corners with tape.

" 'Fun for everyone,' " Violet read. " 'Handicraft booths, refreshments, games, and prizes.' "

"I hope I win a prize," Benny said, scraping up the last of his pie.

"I hope we raise a lot of money," said his grandfather. "Josiah Wade will topple in the middle of the square if we don't replace his base soon."

The statue of Josiah Wade had guarded the center of Greenfield Square for as long as anyone could remember. With his musket at his side, the Revolutionary War hero stood staunchly on a base of granite blocks.

"The base *is* crumbling," Jessie said, looking out the window. "Little pieces of rock have fallen off."

"After the festival, we'll have a new base made for the statue," said Grandfather. "But the town still has to decide whether to move Old Josiah."

"Why move it?" asked Violet. She liked the statue just where it was. The Minuteman wasn't very tall — just a little taller than Grandfather — and it was nice to lean against while eating an ice-cream cone.

"Some people would like to repave the

square," answered Grandfather. "And put a fountain where the statue is."

"Where would the statue go?" Henry asked, returning the roll of tape to Mrs. Turner.

Grandfather shrugged. "That's another question. But first the town must vote whether or not to move the statue. As director of the festival, I'll announce the result the day of the festival."

The ballot box was mounted outside the door of the drugstore. The wooden box had a slot in its hinged lid. Voters slipped ballots into the slot.

"I sent in my ballot," said Mrs. Turner. "Guess which way I voted."

Benny swung around on his stool to face her. "You're not supposed to tell! A vote is secret!"

The other Aldens laughed. Benny was famous for not keeping secrets.

"It's no secret," said the waitress. "Both Mr. Cooke and I want to keep old Josiah in the square where he belongs."

"What about you, Mr. Kirby?" Henry

asked the druggist. "What do you think we should do with the statue? Leave it in the square or move it?"

Mr. Kirby said, "I don't live in this town. So it doesn't matter to me. I'm only here until Mr. Cooke returns."

"You can still vote," Benny told him. He felt everyone should be concerned about the fate of the statue.

Grandfather paid the bill. Then he said to the children, "We've got a lot of festival work to do. We'd better get started."

"At least Mrs. McGregor won't have to feed us lunch," said Jessie. Mrs. McGregor was their housekeeper.

It was so chilly out that Violet had worn her warm, purple jacket. As they went outside, she put her hands in her jacket pockets. Her fingers touched a scrap of paper.

"My pictures!" she said. "I forgot to pick up my photographs. That's the main reason we ate lunch at the drugstore."

Ever since Grandfather gave Violet a camera, she had become the family photographer.

Grandfather handed Violet a ten-dollar bill. "You children go back inside and pick them up. I'm going next door to talk to Miss Pepper about the festival."

"Back again?" Mrs. Turner said when the Aldens pushed through the door. "Need a refill on pie?"

Benny giggled. "Violet forgot to pick up her pictures."

Violet went up to the pharmacy counter. "Here's my ticket, Mr. Kirby."

Mr. Kirby frowned at the ticket. "Yes, there was a shipment from the photo lab earlier this morning. If I can remember where I put those envelopes — "

"They're right where you left them," Mrs. Turner said. "In the back room on the table."

Mr. Kirby disappeared into the back and came out again with a white envelope.

"That'll be nine ninety-five," he told Violet.

"Thank you," she said. After receiving her change, she hurried outside. Looking at her photos was always an exciting moment.

Benny was even more impatient. "Where are the pictures of me?" he asked eagerly, patting Violet on her arm.

"Benny, don't jiggle my arm," Violet said, laughing. "I can't open the envelope."

"Let's go over by the statue," Jessie suggested. "Then we can all look at them."

They moved to the center of the square. The statue's base was crumbling, but it was still a good place to sit.

Violet opened the white envelope and thumbed through her photographs.

"Oh, that's a cute picture of Watch," Jessie commented. Watch was the Alden family's dog.

"This one didn't turn out." Violet wrinkled her nose at a picture of Grandfather. She had accidentally cut off his feet in the shot.

Then she came across something that made her gasp.

"What is it?" Henry asked.

Violet held up a photograph.

"This isn't mine," she said. "I never took this picture."

CHAPTER 2

Mixed-up Pictures

The others gathered around to see Violet's mysterious photograph, which was of the town square. In the center was the Minuteman statue.

"Are you sure you didn't take this?" Jessie asked her sister.

Violet shook her head. "I didn't take any shots in town."

Henry pointed to an odd blank space in the upper half of the photograph. The white space cut off the top of Josiah Wade's upraised musket.

"What happened there?" Henry asked.

Violet knew a little about the developing process. "The film might have been under-exposed," she replied.

"What does that mean?" asked Benny.

"Something could have been wrong with the film. Or maybe there wasn't enough light that day. One thing for sure," Violet added firmly, "this is definitely not my picture."

"Check and see if you're missing a picture," Henry said. "How many were on that roll?"

"Twelve." Violet quickly counted her stack of photographs. "There are thirteen pictures here, so I'm not missing any."

"We should take the extra picture back to the drugstore," Jessie said. "Maybe Mr. Kirby knows who it belongs to."

Just then Grandfather came out of Sylvia's Blooms, the florist shop next door to Cooke's Drugstore. A tall, dark-haired woman walked out with him, talking all the while.

When Grandfather saw the Aldens, he waved them over.

"You children remember Miss Pepper?" he asked.

The Alden children nodded politely and said hello.

Sylvia Pepper was hard to forget, Jessie thought. The woman had shiny black hair pulled back in a tight bun. Red-rimmed glasses framed her snapping dark eyes. Scarlet lipstick matched her silk dress.

Ignoring the children, Sylvia went on with her conversation.

"Don't you agree, Mr. Alden?" she demanded.

"Well — I — " Grandfather began.

"My building is one of the oldest in Greenfield," she said, waving scarlet-tipped fingers as she talked. "It would be logical to put the Minuteman statue in front of *my* store, don't you think?"

"I really can't say," Grandfather said. "It's up to the townspeople to decide whether the statue will be moved."

"I'd plant flowers around the statue," Sylvia rattled on, not listening. "Wouldn't pink petunias be nice?"

Jessie started to giggle. The thought of Josiah Wade, Greenfield's Revolutionary War hero, standing in a tub of pink petunias was just too funny.

When Sylvia looked at her sharply, Jessie turned the laugh into a cough.

"We'll know if the statue will be moved the day of the festival," Grandfather told Sylvia. "Thanks for displaying our poster in your window."

"Don't forget I'm also donating decorations for the festival," Sylvia reminded him. "I hope you'll remember that when you decide where to move the statue."

"We don't want to move the statue," Benny piped up. "We like it in the square. It's always been there."

Sylvia Pepper noticed him for the first time. "Well, it's time for a change. That's the trouble with this town. Everything has been exactly the same for the last two hundred years."

"I think that's what's great about Greenfield," said a new voice. "That's why I moved my business here."

Everyone turned to see a slender woman coming across the square. She wore jeans and a bright orange sweater. A yellow scarf held back her long blond ponytail.

"Miss Wellington," Grandfather greeted. "I don't believe you've met my grandchildren. This is Henry, Jessie, Violet, and Benny."

"Are you the new photographer?" Violet asked. Grandfather had told her a professional photographer was coming to Greenfield.

"Yes, I am. And please call me Dawn," she said. "I don't have my sign up yet, but my studio is open."

Violet stared at the small building on the other side of Cooke's Drugstore. It was nice having a real photographer in town. Maybe Dawn would give her some pointers.

"What do you think about the statue?" Henry asked Dawn. "Should we move it?"

"I'm new here," the young woman replied, "but I believe the statue ought to stay in the square. It belongs there."

"We think so, too!" Benny answered for

the Aldens. "But Miss Pepper doesn't!"

"Benny," Grandfather said. "We're all entitled to our own opinions."

Sylvia Pepper turned a dull red. "Well!" she said huffily. "Some people can stand around gabbing all day, but I've got a business to run!"

With that, she wheeled and went inside her shop, slamming the door.

"Gosh, I hope I didn't make her mad," Dawn said. "I'd like us to be friends."

"I'm sure you will," Grandfather said smoothly. "Sylvia can be a little forceful at times, but that's just her way."

"I have to get back to work myself," said Dawn, heading toward her studio. "Please come see me. I love company."

Grandfather checked his watch. "I still have to visit Reit's Jewelry this afternoon."

"And we have to go back in the drugstore," Violet told him. She hadn't forgotten about the strange photograph.

"When you're finished, meet me in front of town hall," Grandfather said, striding across the square.

The Aldens went back into Cooke's Drugstore. Mrs. Turner was unpacking a carton of first-aid supplies.

Mr. Kirby was talking in a low voice on the phone. When he saw the children, he spoke a few terse words into the receiver and hung up.

Violet put the packet of photographs on his counter. "Mr. Kirby, one of the pictures in this envelope isn't mine."

"What do you mean?" the druggist asked, rather impatiently.

Henry figured Mr. Kirby thought they were wasting his time. "Violet counted her pictures," he said. "She took twelve photographs and there are thirteen in the envelope."

"Let's see it," said Mr. Kirby with a sigh. Violet slid the strange photograph out of the envelope. "Not very interesting, is it?" he remarked critically.

Now Mrs. Turner came over. "I bet that picture fell out when the envelopes got all mixed up."

"Mixed up?" Henry repeated. "What happened?"

"The man who makes the photo deliveries came at a bad time this morning," Mr. Kirby explained. "The store was crowded with people and other deliveries. The photo lab man tripped and dropped the box."

"Envelopes flew everywhere," Mrs. Turner put in, shaking her head. "Mr. Cooke would never leave boxes in the aisle."

Mr. Kirby frowned at her. "Everyone pitched in and helped sort out the envelopes. Several customers had come in to pick up their photographs."

"The picture probably fell out of another envelope," Jessie suggested. "And that person hasn't picked up his or her pictures yet."

Mrs. Turner shook her head. "Nope. The bin where we keep the photo deliveries is empty. Violet, you were the last person to pick up photographs from this delivery."

"Then we don't know who lost this." Violet tucked the mysterious photograph into her own envelope. "If anyone reports a missing picture, please let me know."

"I'm sure no one will claim that dull picture," Mr. Kirby said, turning away.

"Thanks anyway," Henry said. When they left the store, he added, "Boy, that guy's sure not much help. I'll be glad when Mr. Cooke comes back."

Jessie glanced back through the window. Mr. Kirby was dialing the phone again.

"He couldn't wait to get us out of there," she said. "I guess he didn't want us to hear his phone conversation."

"I don't think he likes kids," said Benny as they crossed the square to the town hall building.

Henry agreed. "I think you're right, Benny. Mr. Kirby is one of those grown-ups who is impatient around kids. Like nothing we say or do is important. Some grown-ups are like that."

"I hope you don't mean me," said a cheerful voice behind them. "Am I one of those awful grown-ups?"

Benny recognized the young man first.

"Mr. Bass!" he exclaimed. "You're not awful!"

Rick Bass pretended to wipe his forehead. "Whew! For a minute there, I was worried you thought I was an old grouch."

Jessie laughed. Rick Bass could never be an old grouch. He was too young, for one thing. And he was always smiling. His chestnut hair was the same color as the leaves blowing across the square today.

"When will the museum be open?" she asked him.

Rick shoved his hands deep into the pockets of his denim jacket. "When I was hired, I thought I'd have the Greenfield Historical Museum open in a month. I've been here three months and I'm still digging my way through the artifacts."

"The art — what?" asked Benny.

"Artifacts are objects. Anything that is part of Greenfield's history," replied Rick. "It can be something really old, like a pewter cup from the seventeen-hundreds. Or something not so old, like the first phone book."

Just then Grandfather joined them. "Mr.

Bass," he said. "How is the museum coming along?"

"As I was telling your grandchildren, it's a bigger job than I thought it would be," he replied.

James Alden nodded. "People have been donating items to the historical society for many years. I imagine there's quite a pile of stuff in the town hall basement."

"Yes, sir," Rick agreed. "But I love rooting through old things. You'd be surprised at some discoveries I've made. One is *very* interesting."

Benny was instantly curious. "What is it?"

"Tell us!" Violet urged.

"Not today," said Grandfather. "We must be going."

"We'll be back here tomorrow," Benny informed Rick. "Will you come see us?"

Rick made a thumbs-up sign. "I'll tell you tomorrow."

Benny hated being kept in suspense. "Can you give us a little hint?"

Rick smiled mysteriously. "This town is full of secrets!"

CHAPTER 3

The Hidden Message

"We need a new mystery," Benny said. The four Alden children were sitting and talking in their boxcar, and Benny was feeling restless.

"We have to help Grandfather with the Winter Festival. We don't have time to solve a mystery, too," said Jessie.

She wrote something in a green binder. Knowing that Jessie was organized and responsible, Grandfather had asked her to keep track of preparations for the festival. As

Grandfather's assistant, Jessie kept notes in the festival notebook.

"Can't we do both?" Benny said.

"Well, Benny, mysteries don't just fall out of the sky," Violet said.

"What about your picture?" asked Benny. "That's a mystery."

"Violet's picture is just a weird mistake," said Henry.

Jessie closed her notebook. "We promised to clean the statue today. Is everyone ready?"

"I have the lunch Mrs. McGregor packed us." Violet held up a large wicker picnic basket. She slipped the strange photograph into her basket. Maybe Mr. Kirby had found the rightful owner.

"And I've got the cleaning stuff." Jessie wheeled her bicycle out from the garage. The tote bag containing her notebook swung from her handlebars.

She handed Henry the bucket of cleaning supplies to hang from his handlebars.

Benny climbed on his bike. "Let's go!"

The children pedaled quickly in the crisp morning air to the center of Greenfield.

They parked their bicycles in the lot on one side of the square. Shops and businesses lined two sides. The town hall, with its wide green lawn, occupied the fourth side. In the center of the brick-paved common area stood the statue of Josiah Wade.

Violet wished she had brought her camera. The square looked so pretty today. The copper spire of the town hall gleamed in the bright sunlight.

"What a great day," Henry said.

"Maybe we'll find a new mystery," Benny said hopefully.

"Work first!" Jessie chided gently. Secretly, she also wished they had a new mystery to solve. Life was so much more exciting when they were searching for clues.

They unloaded the cleaning supplies at the base of the statue.

"He sure is dirty." Jessie swiped a finger over one bronze sleeve. "Well, we'll make him clean again."

She handed the bucket to Henry. "Mrs. Turner in the drugstore should let you fill this."

Henry returned a few minutes later with a bucketful of hot water. He squirted in detergent to make suds. Then they each grabbed a brush and began scrubbing.

After working for about a half hour, the children stopped to eat lunch.

After everyone washed their hands at Cooke's Drugstore, Violet passed around turkey and cranberry sauce sandwiches on whole wheat bread. Henry poured them each a cup of hot chocolate from the thermos.

"And we have oatmeal cookies for dessert," Violet said.

"Look how shiny Josiah's boots are," Benny said proudly, munching a carrot stick.

"You did a good job," said Jessie. "That musket is tough, but I've almost got it cleaned."

Across the square, a familiar figure emerged from a side door of the town hall.

"It's Rick!" Benny said, waving excitedly. "Now he'll tell us the secret."

"Looking good," Rick Bass said. "I bet old Josiah loves getting a bath."

Violet offered him an oatmeal cookie.

"You said you know something about the town."

"So I did. Boy, these are good cookies. Please give my compliments to your Mrs. McGregor." Rick's brown eyes crinkled at the corners. He loved to tease.

"Rick!" Benny wailed. "Tell us!"

Rick laughed. "All right! I've kept you in suspense long enough."

The children leaned forward eagerly.

"Josiah Wade," Rick stated, "was not a Minuteman."

"He wasn't a soldier?" Henry asked. "Why is his statue dressed like one?"

"Good question," said Rick. "I think it's a joke the sculptor played on Greenfield."

"What kind of a joke is that?" Violet wondered.

Looking at the children's blank faces, Rick explained, "I've been reading about the history of Greenfield. This statue was created by Franklin Bond."

"Here's the marker," said Jessie, pointing to a small brass plate at the base of the statue.

"It says, 'Sculpted by Franklin A. Bond, June 4, 1855.' "

"Now, think about these dates," Rick told them. "Josiah Wade was born in 1763. The Revolutionary War took place between 1775 and 1783."

Henry did the math quickly in his head. "Josiah was only twelve when the war began."

"Exactly!" Rick was warming to his subject. "Josiah Wade was a teenage boy during the period. He probably remembered the war quite well, but I doubt he actually fought in it."

Benny was confused. "Then why would Franklin Bond make Josiah a soldier if he wasn't?"

"Franklin Bond grew up in Greenfield," replied Rick. "When he was a young boy he knew Josiah Wade. By the time Franklin created the statue, Josiah was an old man. Franklin probably listened to Josiah's stories about the war. Maybe Josiah told Franklin he fought with the patriots."

Henry studied the bronze statue. "If Josiah really wasn't a soldier, then that's a good joke on us!"

"Josiah Wade helped form the town of Greenfield, so he deserved a statue in his honor," Rick said. "A man looks more important in a uniform. But I doubt Josiah Wade ever wore one."

Since it was lunchtime, the square was growing busy. Sylvia Pepper came out of her florist's shop to inspect the Aldens' cleaning job.

"Not bad," she said critically. "I don't suppose there's anything you can do about that crumbly old base."

"We've been trying," Henry told her. "But little stones keep dropping off. It'll be great when old Josiah gets a new base."

"It would be even better if the statue were moved," Sylvia said. She eyed Rick Bass. "You're the town historian, aren't you?"

"Actually," he corrected, "I'm the curator for the new museum."

"Well, don't you agree the statue should be moved? It just clutters the square," Sylvia said. "My building is the oldest on the square, so it should be in front of my shop."

Rick shook his head. "If the town wants to move the statue, I believe it should be part of the museum."

"Bury it in the basement of the town hall!" Sylvia said shrilly. "What a ridiculous idea!"

"I've got to go back to work," Rick told the Aldens abruptly. "Thanks for the cookie."

Violet could tell Rick didn't like Sylvia. She didn't blame him. Sylvia Pepper wasn't very friendly.

Dawn Wellington joined the group. Today her blond ponytail was tied back with a blue ribbon that matched her eyes.

"The statue really sparkles!" she said.

"We were just talking about where it should be moved," Sylvia said.

"But we don't know *if* it will be moved," Dawn pointed out. "The vote won't be announced until Saturday. I put in my ballot!"

"Anyone with any sense will agree the statue should be moved." Sylvia waved her arm, her silver bracelets jangling. "We want a nice, modern fountain there."

"Not all of us," Dawn said. "I like the square just the way it is."

"What do you know?" Sylvia retorted. "You've just come here." With that, she flounced across the square to her shop.

Dawn bit her lip. "I didn't mean to make her mad."

"She's awfully touchy," Jessie observed.

"I shouldn't repeat gossip," Dawn said, "but Mrs. Turner told me that Sylvia's shop isn't doing very well. I guess that's why she's a little testy."

Just then Violet remembered the photograph in the picnic basket.

"I have a strange picture. Maybe you could tell us about it." She pulled the mysterious photo out and handed it to Dawn.

"See? It's got that funny blank spot near the top," Benny pointed out.

Dawn squinted at the picture. "Hmmmm," she said thoughtfully. "I'd like to try something in my studio. May I borrow your picture, Violet?"

"Sure. Can we come, too?" Violet asked.

"Of course." Dawn led the way into her photography studio.

They walked past the front room, and through a door with a red light over the top.

The windowless room contained sinks and counters filled with strange-looking equipment. A single red bulb overhead provided the only light.

"It's sure dark in here," Benny remarked.

"This is my darkroom," Dawn explained. "This is where I develop pictures. Bright light ruins unexposed film, so I work with little illumination."

Dawn dipped the strange photo into a pan of liquid. Then she turned on a small lamp attached to her counter. Pushing the metal shade to one side, she held the photo over the bare lightbulb.

"Just as I thought," she said. "Watch carefully."

Slowly, words appeared in the blank space on the photograph.

CHAPTER 4

Caught Red-handed!

Everyone stood still in the dark-room. They stared at the sticklike letters forming before their eyes.

The letters spelled out a single sentence:

MOVE IT THE DAY BEFORE

Benny, who was just learning to read, repeated the strange words in an awed whisper.

"Amazing!" Henry murmured.

"How did you know there was something written there?" Violet asked Dawn.

The photographer turned off the small lamp and flipped a wall switch. The dark-room was suddenly bright.

"The paper tipped me off," Dawn said, waving the photograph to dry it. "The texture didn't feel right."

Jessie touched the photograph. "It feels like ordinary paper to me."

Dawn smiled. "I learned some tricks in one of my photography classes in college. We would coat a special paper with a chemical solution. With another chemical, we would write or draw on this treated paper. Only you wouldn't see it."

"So the space would look blank," Henry said.

"Exactly," Dawn said. "To make the words or drawing appear, we simply dipped the paper in water. And then held it over a light."

"Just like the invisible writing spies use!" Benny exclaimed. "We have a spy in Greenfield!"

Dawn laughed. "I don't know about a spy, but someone knows a lot about photography.

The paper that picture is printed on is unusual. It's not used for ordinary developing."

"Where would paper like that come from?" asked Jessie. "I mean, Violet's pictures were printed on regular paper."

"You can request it," Dawn replied. "You can order a certain type of paper when you drop off your roll of film."

Violet nodded. "On the envelope you check off the size of your prints and how many. I always order four-by-six prints and only one set. Then if one of my pictures turns out really well, I might order another copy."

"Those are called reprints," Dawn told her. "The big developing labs do all sorts of special services."

Jessie stared at the equipment in the darkroom. "I'm confused. How did that strange picture get in Violet's photographs?"

"Good question." Dawn tugged her ponytail over one shoulder. "Basically, a person drops film off at a store. The store sends the roll of film — along with lots of others — away to a laboratory. The lab develops the film, then sends the prints back to the store."

"So the mix-up could have happened at the lab," Henry guessed.

"Or at the drugstore," Dawn added, still holding the photograph. "Would you mind if I kept this, Violet? It's such a neat example."

Violet hesitated. She liked Dawn, but she didn't want to give up the message photograph. Not until they found out more.

"I'm trying to find the person who lost this," she said finally. "Mr. Kirby said he'd let me know if anyone asks for it."

Dawn reluctantly handed the photograph to Violet. "If nobody claims the picture, maybe you'd let me have it."

"Thanks a lot," Violet said. "You've been a big help."

"Yeah," said Benny. "We never would have found the message."

Dawn opened the door to the front room. "I'll see you kids around. I'm taking pictures for a souvenir booklet about the town square."

"We're having a photo booth at the festival," Violet said.

Jessie nodded. "People are going to pose by Josiah's statue."

Dawn smiled. "Good! You can't have too many photographers at a special event."

Outside, the Aldens bubbled over with excitement.

"A secret message!" Benny whooped.

"But what does it mean?" Henry asked. "Move what? The day before what?"

"Who was supposed to get this message?" Violet put in.

"Who sent it?" Jessie wondered.

"And how," Benny added, "did the picture get into Violet's envelope?"

Jessie sighed, adjusting the strap of her tote bag. "Looks like you were right all along, Benny."

He grinned. "I knew we'd find another mystery!"

The children talked about the new mystery as they finished cleaning the statue. Jessie was buffing the small brass plate when Grandfather came by.

"Old Josiah never looked better," he

praised. He held up two cans of red paint. "I found some leftover paint in the garage. How about repainting the benches?"

"Sure," Henry said. "We like to paint."

When Grandfather left, the children painted the benches. They even had enough paint for the trash cans.

As they were cleaning the brushes, Jessie said, "I wish we knew more about that photograph. I can't stop thinking about it."

"We know the delivery man from the photo lab dropped his bag of envelopes in the drugstore," said Violet. "The photograph probably fell out of someone's envelope — "

"And accidentally got put into your envelope," Henry finished. "How can we find out who else had pictures in that delivery?"

"Easy." Benny wiped his hands on a rag. "Why don't we go in the drugstore and ask Mr. Kirby?"

Cooke's Drugstore was crowded with mid-afternoon shoppers. Jessie recognized Sylvia Pepper. She also caught a glimpse of Rick Bass spinning a rack of greeting cards.

Henry went up to the pharmacy counter. "Excuse me," he said politely. "Has anyone asked about the missing picture?"

"What missing picture?" As usual, Mr. Kirby was busy.

"This picture. The one that was in my envelope," Violet reminded him.

She took the message photograph from her basket. She flashed it briefly, with her thumb over the blank space. She didn't want Mr. Kirby to see the message.

"Oh, that photograph." The pharmacist drew his bushy brows together in a frown. "I told you kids to forget about it. One dumb photograph isn't important."

But Violet knew the photograph *was* important.

"We'd like to track down the owner," she said. "Could you tell us who was in the store yesterday morning? When the delivery man dropped the bag of envelopes?"

Mr. Kirby made an impatient noise. "Do you kids really think I can remember everyone who was in the store yesterday morning? I don't even know the people around here.

I'm just the substitute. Now I'm very busy."

Henry took the hint. Mr. Kirby was always too busy to bother with "kids."

"One more thing," he said. "Could we leave our paint supplies with you? We'll pick them up tomorrow."

Mr. Kirby flapped his hand. "Yeah, sure. I'll take care of it. Just leave the stuff outside the store."

"Maybe Mrs. Turner will help us," Benny said, leading the way to the counter.

Mrs. Turner laughed when she saw the Aldens. "Look at those red hands!"

"We've been painting benches," Benny said. He looked down at his red-smeared fingers.

Henry spoke up. "Mrs. Turner, could you tell us who was in the store yesterday when the photo delivery man dropped the bag? We asked Mr. Kirby, but he couldn't help us."

The waitress shook her head sympathetically. "You have to forgive Mr. Kirby. He was hoping to end his stay in Greenfield, but Mr. Cooke called to say he'd be gone another week." Mrs. Turner lowered her voice. "I think he's trying to find a job in another town. He keeps phoning to set up interviews."

"I don't know why he doesn't like it here," Jessie said. "Greenfield is a friendly town." Much friendlier than Mr. Kirby, she thought.

Henry got back to the question. "Do you remember who was in here yesterday?"

"Sure do. Two of them are here right now." Mrs. Turner nodded toward the back of the store. "Sylvia Pepper was one. She made a big fuss because we don't carry her brand of toothpaste."

"Who else?" Benny prodded.

"The young man who's running the museum," the waitress replied. "What's his name?"

"Rick Bass," Jessie supplied.

"And that new photographer next door. Dawn Wellington," added the waitress.

Violet drew in a breath. Dawn had never mentioned being in the drugstore the morning of the photo mix-up.

"The place was a madhouse," Mrs. Turner

went on. "No wonder the man from the lab dropped his delivery sack."

A line of people waited at the cash register by the door. Sylvia Pepper tapped her foot impatiently. Rick Bass was also in line. Mrs. Turner left to take care of the customers.

"Did you hear that?" Henry said. "Both Sylvia Pepper and Rick Bass were in here yesterday morning."

"Dawn, too," said Benny.

"Any one of them could have picked up pictures they had developed," Jessie stated.

"Not Dawn," Violet said. "She develops her own film. Why would she send her photos away to a lab?"

"But she really wanted to keep your message photo," Henry reminded her. "I wonder why she was so interested."

Violet nodded. Henry was right. Maybe Dawn was the one who sent the message photo. Or was she the one who was supposed to receive it?

Benny was thinking that a hot fudge sundae would hit the spot. "Mysteries sure make me hungry," he hinted.

Jessie smiled. "Sorry, Benny. Mrs. Turner is busy. And we have to get home."

The children worked their way through the crowd clustered near the front door.

As Jessie put her hand on the door to push it open, she felt the strap on her tote bag dig sharply into her shoulder. A second, harder jerk nearly knocked her off balance.

She whirled to look back, but there were too many people leaving the store. That yank was deliberate.

Someone had tried to steal her bag!

"Henry! Did you see who tried to grab my bag?" asked Jessie.

"No, I didn't. Maybe it was just an accident," said Henry.

"Maybe," said Jessie. But she doubted it.

CHAPTER 5

The Phantom in the Town Square

"Brrr!" said Jessie, buttoning her jacket up to her chin. "It sure is cold!"

Winter was definitely in the air at the Farm Meadow Nursery. Swags of greenery were looped along the fence. Tiny white lights twinkled in the evergreen trees.

The Aldens had driven to the nursery with their grandfather to pick up decorations for the festival. Today they would begin decorating the square with greenery. The festival was only three days away.

"It's supposed to be cold," Benny told Jessie as they walked among the potted spruce and fir trees. "Who ever heard of a hot Winter Festival?"

Jessie held tightly to the strap of her tote bag. Even though there were few people around, she wasn't taking any chances.

Benny saw his sister grip the strap. "Are you sure somebody tried to grab your bag yesterday?" he asked.

"Positive," she replied. "Whoever it was pulled hard. That person definitely wanted this bag. But the only thing I carry in it is the festival notebook."

"Why would anyone want your notebook?" Benny asked.

"I don't know," Jessie replied. She'd be glad when the festival was over. Being her grandfather's assistant was a lot of responsibility.

Violet caught up to them. She had been taking pictures. Now she snapped Benny standing beside a small fir tree.

"The tree is just your size!" she said, laughing.

The three of them found Henry and

Grandfather loading holly branches into the trunk of their car.

"Ouch!" Henry cried. "The points on this holly are going right through my gloves."

"Be careful," Grandfather warned. "Let's load the wreaths next."

The Aldens stacked pine wreaths on the backseat. A bushel of pine cones was placed on the floor.

"The town square is going to look so pretty," Jessie said as they all squeezed into the car.

They drove from the nursery to town. To-day Grandfather had special permission to drive up the lane into the square. Once they were in the square, everyone hopped out of the car.

"Let's pile the greens next to the statue," Grandfather directed, unlocking the trunk. "The rest of my decorating committee should be here soon."

Benny was staring at the statue. His mouth fell open. "Look!" he cried.

Jessie gasped.

"Oh, no!" Violet exclaimed.

The Minuteman had been painted a bright, cheery red. Red paint coated the statue, from his bronze toes to the top of his musket.

"Oh, my," Grandfather remarked.

Dawn Wellington rushed into the square. "Mr. Alden," she said breathlessly. "I tried to call you, but your housekeeper said you were out. Isn't it awful?"

"A terrible prank," Grandfather agreed.

Just then, Mrs. Turner came out of the drugstore. "Mr. Alden! When I got to work this morning, that's what I saw!"

Violet noticed a red-smeared can in one of the trash cans.

"Here are the paint cans," she said.

Henry turned to the waitress. "We asked Mr. Kirby if he could store the cans for us until today. He told us to leave them outside and he would put them away."

"I left early yesterday," said Mrs. Turner. "I remember seeing your paint things by the door."

"That's where we left them." Henry

touched one of the statue's red-painted boots. "It's still sticky. It wasn't painted that long ago."

"Probably early this morning," Grandfather said. "Good thing it's water-based paint. Since it's not dry yet, it should wash off."

"I'll get some soap and water," Dawn offered, and dashed across the square to her studio. She returned with two buckets filled with hot, soapy water and several scrub brushes.

The Aldens got right to work. With Dawn and Grandfather's help, the statue soon went from tomato red to its normal bronze color.

"Did you see anyone this morning?" Henry asked Dawn when they were finished. "Anybody who looked suspicious?"

She shook her blond ponytail. "No one. I came in early because I wanted to get started on the souvenir booklet. I planned to take shots of the square in the morning light. What a shock to see this bright red statue!"

"Well, it's over and done with," Grandfather said. "Let's get on with the festival preparations."

But before anyone could move, Sylvia Pepper flew out from her shop. "Do you see that?" she demanded, pointing to her doorway with its address numbers.

Benny realized immediately what was wrong. "The numbers are backward," he said. "It should be two-one-one, not one-one-two."

"Exactly!" Sylvia screeched. "When I got to work this morning, someone had switched the address numbers. Everyone's addresses are wrong!"

Sure enough, the brass numbers over every shop door were out of order. Dawn's shop, number 209, was now 902. All around the square, the address numbers were mixed up.

"I don't understand," said Dawn. "I thought Greenfield was a nice, quiet town. That's why I moved here."

"It *is* a nice place," Violet said, defending her town. "These things have never happened before."

"Well, it doesn't seem very nice now," said Sylvia. "When my lease is up, I might look for another location for Sylvia's Blooms."

James Alden put out a calming hand. "Let's not panic," he said. "This is just a practical joke."

Dawn looked uneasy. "But the person did all this without being seen. It's like a phantom."

"The phantom of Greenfield square," Henry said. It *was* strange that no one saw the vandal.

"The culprit is probably miles away," said Grandfather.

Benny wasn't so sure. But there was a way to find out.

Red paint was hard to clean off. At home last night, he had to scrub a long time to remove the red paint from under his fingernails. The person who painted the statue must have red fingernails, too.

"Do you want us to look for whoever did it?" he asked his grandfather.

"Thanks, Benny. But I think we should

work on the festival. I'll fix the address numbers right now."

"We'll unload the decorations," Henry offered.

The Aldens walked over to the car. Grandfather fetched a small toolbox and went back to Sylvia's shop. The children gathered armloads of greenery. They heaped the decorations at the base of Josiah Wade.

"Something strange is going on," Jessie remarked as she straightened an evergreen garland. "Who would paint the statue?"

"Or switch the address numbers?" Henry wondered. "Why mess up the square when the festival is just days away?"

Benny carefully placed holly branches on the brick pavement. "Maybe somebody doesn't want the festival."

"Who wouldn't want a fun celebration?" asked Violet. "And for such a good cause, too."

"I guess everyone doesn't feel the way we do about our town," Henry said, glancing at Cooke's Drugstore. "I'd like to ask Mr. Kirby what he did with our paint cans."

When the last wreath was stacked neatly beside the statue, Grandfather came over.

"Since we've been working extra hard today, let's have lunch in the drugstore," he suggested.

"I sure could use a piece of Mrs. Turner's apple pie." Benny had eaten all the crackers Mrs. McGregor packed in his knapsack.

Jessie laughed. "Well, you'll have to last long enough to eat a sandwich first."

Inside the drugstore, Henry said to Jessie, "Could you order me a tuna sandwich? I want to talk to Mr. Kirby."

"I'm coming, too," Violet said.

Mr. Kirby didn't look happy to see them. "What can I do for you?" he asked Henry.

"Yesterday we left some paint supplies," Henry said. "We asked you to keep them for us overnight. You said to leave them outside and you would bring them in."

"Right," Mr. Kirby said. "When I locked up last night, I didn't see any paint cans. I thought you had taken them home after all."

Returning to their stools, Henry whispered to Violet, "Somebody took the paint cans! Then that person came back after everyone was gone and painted the statue."

"But who?" asked Violet.

After apple pie with cinnamon sauce, Mrs. Turner's new creation, the Aldens returned to the square.

"Where are the people who are supposed to help decorate?" Jessie asked Grandfather. She flipped through her festival notebook. "Dawn Wellington, Rick Bass, Sylvia Pepper, Mr. Ames the hardware store owner, and Ms. Reit from the jewelry store are on the committee."

Grandfather checked his watch. "They were supposed to meet here at two-thirty. Maybe they forgot. I have a meeting, but first I'll pop into the shops and remind everyone."

"We'll do that, Grandfather," Violet said. She was afraid her grandfather was working too hard on this festival.

Henry took off his jacket and left it at the base of the statue. The chilly morning had warmed up.

"We'll leave our things here. We won't be gone that long," he said.

Jessie glanced around the empty square. She could look through any shop window and see the statue. Her bag should be safe here for a few minutes.

The children walked around, reminding the members of the decorating committee. Only Rick Bass wasn't available. He wasn't in the museum in the basement of the town hall. No one had seen him all day.

When they were on their way back to the statue, Jessie noticed something odd. Her tote bag was lying in a different spot from where she had left it. She ran to check it. Her notebook was still there.

Benny was hunting for his knapsack. "I put it right here." He finally found it under a pile of holly.

"Someone's been in our things," Jessie told Henry.

Henry picked up his jacket. Sure enough, the pockets were turned inside out. "Someone went through my jacket."

Violet looked around for her camera bag.

"Oh, no," she moaned. "I left my bag here and it's gone!"

CHAPTER 6

The Phantom Strikes Again

"Are you sure your camera bag is missing?" Jessie asked Violet. "Maybe you took it into the drugstore."

Violet shook her head. "I left it here, with our coats and things. I can't believe someone would steal it."

"Well, somebody did," Henry said grimly.

Benny hated to see his sister so upset. "Don't worry, Violet. Let's go look in the drugstore, just in case."

But Mrs. Turner wasn't able to help them.

"I know that gray bag of yours," she said to Violet. "You didn't bring it with you today. I'm sure you just left your bag at home."

Violet smiled weakly, but she felt awful. Her camera wasn't at home; she'd been taking pictures most of the day. She should have been more responsible with her belongings.

As the Aldens went back outside, they met Dawn Wellington on the sidewalk.

"Hi, kids," she said cheerfully.

Sylvia Pepper came across the square. She brought a box of red ribbons. "For the wreaths," she said.

A few seconds later, Mr. Ames and Ms. Reit joined Sylvia.

"Greenfield Decorating Committee reporting for duty," Dawn joked, giving a snappy salute. "All present and accounted for."

"Everyone but Rick Bass," Jessie said. "I wonder where he is."

"He's probably just late," Henry said. "We'll ask if anyone has seen Violet's camera bag."

But no one had.

Violet had hoped someone had seen her bag by the statue and taken it inside for safe-keeping. But her camera seemed to be gone forever.

Benny inspected everyone's fingernails. He didn't see any telltale red paint. Sylvia Pepper always had bright red fingernails.

The rest of the afternoon, they draped garlands around shop windows. Each door was graced with a ribbon-tied pine wreath. Even the lampposts sported sprigs of holly.

When they were finished, the decorators stood back to survey the square.

"Too plain," Sylvia said, frowning. "I'm going to add flowers and bows to my door."

"I like the simple wreaths," Dawn said. "It looks like New England. I think Josiah Wade would approve."

The mention of Josiah Wade made Jessie think about Rick Bass. He hadn't shown up. Had something happened to the museum curator?

Benny also glanced at the statue, tall and stately in the late afternoon sun. If only the Minuteman could talk. He would ask Josiah who took his sister's camera bag. But he knew statues couldn't speak.

When he heard about the theft that evening at dinner, Grandfather was very understanding.

"These things happen," he told Violet. "When the festival is over, we'll get you another camera."

"And we won't stop looking for the stolen one," Henry promised. "Your camera just didn't walk away."

"But I'm supposed to take pictures at the festival," Violet protested. "That's my job at the Alden booth. Without my camera, we'll have to do something else for the festival."

She hated to let Grandfather down. She knew he had a lot on his mind. The man who was supposed to play the clown had gotten sick. Grandfather needed to find another clown.

Benny had an idea. "You're a good artist, Violet. Maybe you could *draw* people in front of the statue."

"Thanks, Benny," Violet said, smiling.

"But I doubt I can draw that well."

The phone rang.

Grandfather got up to answer it. "Don't worry," he assured Violet as he left the dining room. "We'll think of a solution. We Aldens always solve our problems."

Mrs. McGregor came in with a freshly baked layer cake.

"It's butter pecan," she said before Benny could ask. She cut thick slices for each of the children. "You can think better after you've eaten cake warm from the oven."

"Delicious!" Jessie praised, licking brown-sugar frosting from her fork.

Henry ate slowly. He was thinking about Violet's missing camera bag. So many strange things had happened in the town square lately. Was one person causing all the trouble?

Just then Grandfather came back. "That was certainly a strange call," he said quietly.

"What was it about?" asked Henry. He sensed his grandfather's concern.

"The person on the other end said, 'Tell

the town council to put the statue in the museum, or else!' "

"That *is* strange," Benny agreed. "Who was it?"

Grandfather shrugged. "It was a man. His voice was muffled, but . . . well, it sounded a little like Rick Bass."

A chill rippled down Jessie's spine. Rick was supposed to help decorate that afternoon and he never showed up. Was he planning to make a threatening phone call instead?

When the phone rang again, everyone jumped.

"Don't answer it," Violet begged.

"I have to find out who it is," Grandfather said, leaving the table once more.

The Aldens were tense until their grandfather returned.

"Was it that man again?" Benny asked.

"No." James Alden heaved a big sigh. "It was Ron Shiplett, the manager of the construction crew I hired to build the festival booths."

Jessie opened her notebook, her pencil

posed over the page. "What did he want? I'll write it down."

"He's canceling!" Grandfather answered. "I have no idea where I'll get another construction crew on such short notice. So much has gone wrong. The festival is only two days away and I need a new clown *and* a new construction crew!"

For the first time, Grandfather really sounded worried.

The next morning, Grandfather dropped the children in town.

"I'll be back soon," he told them. "I'll pick you up by the town hall." Then he drove off to an appointment.

The Aldens were supposed to find someone to play the clown. They planned to ask around the shops.

But when they stepped into the square, a shocking sight met them.

The town square was a mess.

Their decorations had been torn down. Scraps of boughs and battered wreaths lay scattered around the square. Trampled holly

had been stuffed in the trash cans.

"Oh, no!" Violet exclaimed.

"The phantom strikes again." Henry picked up a twisted wreath. "Grandfather will have to go back to the nursery and buy more greenery."

"Maybe we can save some of this," Benny suggested.

He walked over to the trash can near the town hall and lifted out a pile of holly.

Then he gave a cry. The others ran over.

"Look what I found!" Benny reached in and pulled out a familiar gray bag.

"My camera!" Violet unzipped the bag. Her camera was still there. Even her rolls of film were still stored in special pockets along the padded sides.

Jessie set her tote bag behind the bench.

"Why would someone take Violet's case and then put it in the trash?" she asked.

Henry was puzzled, too. "If the thief didn't want the camera, then what did he want?"

Violet drew in a breath. "The message photograph! I put it in the pocket with my film." She hastily checked the bag. "And it's missing!"

Henry snapped his fingers. "That explains why our things were gone through yesterday. Someone wanted that photograph bad enough to steal it!"

"Was it the person who sent the photograph?" Jessie mused. "Or the person who was supposed to receive it?"

"How come no one ever sees anything?" Henry wanted to know. "The statue was painted, the door numbers switched, and our decorations were ruined — all by an invisible person!"

"It's the phantom of Greenfield Square," Benny said.

Jessie shook her head. "It's no ghost. The person is too smart to get caught, that's all."

At that moment, Rick Bass sauntered up. "Hey, guys," he greeted. "Isn't it a shame about the decorations?" He clucked his tongue.

"Where were you yesterday?" Jessie asked.

"I got tied up," Rick replied. "Sorry I couldn't make it."

Benny wondered why Rick kept his hands in the pockets of his denim jacket. Could he be hiding something, like red paint under his nails?

Henry noticed this, too. "I have a jacket just like yours," he said to Rick. "I wore it yesterday."

"I know," Rick said, embarrassed. "I came out to mail a letter. I saw your jacket by the statue and thought it was mine. When I put it on, I realized it was too small."

Part of the mystery was explained. But Henry still didn't know who had taken Violet's camera bag.

Jessie was thinking the same thing. "Did you see anybody around the statue yesterday afternoon?" she asked.

He shook his head. "Not a soul. Hey, I found something I want to show you guys."

"Where is it?" Jessie asked. She wasn't sure she trusted Rick.

"In the museum," Rick replied.

"We have to meet Grandfather soon," said Henry.

"This will only take a minute. Follow me."

Rick led the way through a side door of the town hall. He pulled the door shut and skipped down a flight of steep stairs. At the bottom, the cement landing was musty-smelling.

Violet sneezed.

"It is kind of moldy in here," Rick said apologetically. "Old buildings are damp."

He unlocked a second door. Leaving this door open, Rick entered the shadowed interior.

The Alden children followed cautiously.

"Watch your step," Rick warned.

Violet couldn't see much. Dim light filtered through two narrow windows near the ceiling.

She turned around, bumping into a dark, hulking shape.

"Oh," she said, startled.

CHAPTER 7

The Greenfield Spy

"Violet! What is it?" Henry cried, next to her.

But Violet was frozen in the darkness. She was afraid to move. The dark shape did not move, either.

"Wait, I'll get the light." Rick pulled the chain of an overhead light.

When she saw the "monster," Violet giggled nervously. It was a black wool cape thrown over a coatrack.

"I thought it was a person," she said.

"That's Mr. Phineas T. Goodbody's opera

cape," Rick said. "He donated it to the historical society many years ago. I haven't found a place for it yet."

Jessie could see why. Every square inch of the cramped space was crowded with objects. Hats topped towers of books. Papers overflowed from a huge wooden desk. Unpacked boxes and bags sat on the floor.

"Wow!" Benny exclaimed. "Look at all these neat things!"

"And I have to sort every piece of it," Rick said, riffling through a stack of papers. "Here's what I wanted you guys to see."

Carefully he smoothed an old yellowed sheet. It was a drawing. Faint writing had been scribbled above the figure of a soldier.

"That's the Minuteman statue," Jessie said.

Rick nodded. "This is Franklin Bond's original sketch for the statue. Can you read what he wrote at the top?"

Benny tilted his head. "I can read some, but this writing is too squiggly."

Rick laughed. "Yes, old script is hard to read. Franklin says that Josiah Wade was a

teenage spy during the Revolutionary War. Josiah carried secret messages in the hollow buttons of his coat!"

"A spy!" Benny cried. "So there was a spy in Greenfield!"

"That was a long time ago," Henry said meaningfully. He knew Benny was thinking about the person who sent the message photograph. Now that the photograph had been stolen, they should be suspicious of everyone, including Rick Bass.

"You were right," Violet said to Rick. "Josiah wasn't a soldier. But why did Franklin Bond make a soldier statue?"

"I think it was his little joke on the town," replied Rick. "Franklin wanted to be a great artist. He accepted the statue job because he needed money."

"I thought Mr. Bond liked Josiah Wade," Jessie remarked.

"He did," Rick agreed. "They were great friends, despite their age difference. According to the notes on this drawing, Josiah gave Franklin a gift when he was a boy."

"What was it?" Benny asked.

Rick shook his head. "Franklin doesn't say. I think he liked keeping secrets. But I believe I can find the present."

"Where?" asked Violet, glancing around the cluttered room. How could anyone find anything in this mess?

Rick tapped the drawing. "See that little box penciled lightly near the statue?"

Violet bent closer. Now she could read the old-fashioned handwriting. " 'The Statue's Secret,' " she read aloud. "What does that mean?"

Benny felt a current of air hit his face. Had someone opened the outer door?

Rick grinned broadly. "I'll bet a piece of Mrs. Turner's apple pie that Josiah's gift is hidden inside the statue! That little box is a secret compartment!"

Before Benny could say anything, Dawn Wellington and Sylvia Pepper came into the museum. Benny wondered if they had heard Rick talking about the statue's secret.

Rick jumped with surprise. "Ladies," he said. "What can I do for you?"

"We're looking for Mr. Alden," Dawn replied. "Is he here?"

"No," Henry said. "Grandfather is still trying to find a construction crew."

"That's what I wanted to see him about," Sylvia said in her bossy tone. "I heard the original contractors backed out, so I hired another crew. They'll be here tomorrow."

Jessie was amazed. Sylvia Pepper didn't seem like the type to help Grandfather with the festival.

"And I wanted to tell Mr. Alden that we can salvage most of the decorations," Dawn said. "We'll just make the garlands shorter. Sylvia and I can fix the wreaths."

"This is terrific," Rick said. He walked over to them, leaving the drawing on the table. "Mr. Alden will be pleased. He's worked so hard on the festival."

Rick and Dawn began talking about the vandalism of the past few days. Sylvia moved over to the table.

Jessie watched her. There was something odd about that woman.

Just then Sylvia dropped her purse. Its contents spilled all over the table.

"I'm so clumsy," she muttered. As she picked up lipsticks and coins, she stared intently at the drawing. The woman's eyes grew round.

She acts like she's seen that drawing before, Jessie thought.

But how was that possible? Rick Bass had only discovered Franklin Bond's papers yesterday. How could Sylvia Pepper have seen that drawing before?

And how, she wondered, did Sylvia know the construction crew had canceled?

"Now we have two mysteries to solve," Benny said. "The one about the message photograph. And now the mystery of the statue."

Jessie tied a ribbon around a bag of oatmeal cookies. "Don't forget the strange things happening in the town square lately," she said.

"Okay. Three mysteries." Benny took a fistful of cookies from the large tin on the kitchen table. He put three in a small plastic sack, then ate one.

"Benny Alden!" Violet scolded, laughing. "We can't sell a bag with a cookie missing. People want to buy a full bag."

"Mrs. McGregor's oatmeal cookies are worth more than four for a quarter," Henry said. "But Violet's right, Benny. Make sure four cookies go in each sack."

"And no more in your stomach," Jessie added.

The Aldens had been working since dinner, helping Mrs. McGregor make her famous oatmeal-raisin cookies to sell at the refreshment booth at the Winter Festival.

The housekeeper retired to her room when the children volunteered to bag the cookies.

"I hope we make lots of money from Mrs. McGregor's cookies," Benny said.

"And from the pictures Violet will take," Henry added. "There should be enough money to fix the statue's base."

"Do you think the town will vote to move the statue?" Violet asked.

"Who knows?" Henry shrugged. "Grandfather will bring the ballot box home and count the votes himself tomorrow night. And on Saturday, he'll announce the result."

"Grandfather is working awfully hard on the festival," Benny said. "We haven't seen him much all day."

"That's because he's busy talking to people," Henry explained. "It's a big job, putting on this festival."

"I'm glad we're able to help," said Violet. She plopped another bag in the carton on the floor.

"He's been gone since dinner," Jessie said, glancing at the clock. "I hope he doesn't get home too late tonight."

"You've kept Grandfather organized," Henry said to her.

"Well, I write everything down," Jessie said modestly. "And put it in the notebook." Suddenly she clapped her hand over her mouth.

Violet looked at her in concern. "What is it, Jess? What's wrong?"

"The festival notebook," she whispered. "I left it in town!"

"It'll be okay," Henry assured her. "We'll get it tomorrow."

Jessie shook her head. "No. I can't leave it there, Henry. The person who's been wrecking the square might find it. He could use it to do more damage."

Violet stared at Henry. "Jessie's right. We can't take that chance."

"Let's go get it," Henry suggested.

"Grandfather's not home yet," Jessie said. "I hate to cause him more trouble."

"I didn't mean in the car," Henry said. "You and I can ride our bikes. It won't take long. Benny and Violet, you should stay here and let Mrs. McGregor know that we'll be right back."

Quickly, Henry and Jessie scrambled into their jackets and slipped out the back door.

Jessie was glad when they reached the lane leading into the town square. She parked her bike next to Henry's.

"Where did you leave the notebook?" asked Henry.

"Behind the bench by the town hall," Jessie replied, pulling her jacket tighter. A sharp wind had sprung up. "I put it there when Benny found Violet's camera. Then, with all that talk about the hidden compartment in the statue, I forgot about it."

"We'll get it now and hurry home," Henry said, heading across the pavement.

"It's so quiet out here," Jessie said, listening to the soft thud of her sneakers on the bricks.

The town square was lit by lampposts at all four corners. The tall, dark Minuteman statue was illuminated by a spotlight.

Then another, stronger light slashed across the square.

Henry stopped. "Someone's there!" he whispered. "He has a flashlight!"

The light switched off abruptly, leaving the square shadowy.

Jessie saw the figure run away from the statue. It was a small person, with a flowing ponytail.

It looked like Dawn Wellington.

CHAPTER 8

A Scrap of Red

"Quick!" Henry said, grabbing Jessie's wrist, and the two flew across the pavement.

It was getting darker and the town hall cast a long, spooky shadow. At last they reached the bench.

Jessie's tote bag containing her notebook was leaning against one wrought-iron leg. She snatched it up.

"I wonder if that person was looking for your notebook, too," Henry said as they hurried toward the parking lot.

"I don't know," Jessie said over her shoulder.

Their footsteps fell softly on the worn bricks, but something didn't sound right. Henry stopped, causing Jessie to stop, too.

Behind them, more footsteps rang out, then died.

"Someone's back there!" Jessie whispered. "We're being followed!"

Henry thought so, too. "Let's get on our bikes and head home," he said quietly.

Henry opened the back door for Jessie. Grandfather hadn't returned and Mrs. McGregor was in her room. Benny, Violet, and Watch were waiting in the living room. Watch thumped his tail in greeting.

Jessie buried her face in the dog's thick fur. She was glad to be home.

"Who was that person lurking around the statue?" she asked Henry.

"It was definitely a woman," said Henry. "It looked like Dawn, but why would she run away? She could see it was just us."

"What about that other person?" Jessie asked. "The one who was following us."

"You don't think that was Dawn coming back?" asked Henry.

Jessie shook her head. "The footsteps sounded different. Heavier."

"If you're right, then maybe we scared off the phantom of Greenfield Square," Henry said. "But we still don't know who it is. But one thing is for sure: we should keep an eye on Rick Bass, Sylvia Pepper, and Dawn Wellington. They've all acted strange."

"Tomorrow we can look for clues. You two can help us, okay?" Jessie suggested to Violet and Benny. "Maybe we'll find something around the statue."

"Good idea," Henry said. "We have to work on the festival anyway."

The festival was the day after tomorrow. Henry wondered if the event would take place after all.

The next morning the Aldens rode into town with Grandfather.

"We have a lot of work to do today," James Alden said. "It's my job to keep everyone on schedule."

"And it's my job to keep *you* on schedule," said Jessie. The notebook was close by her side. She wasn't going to let it out of her sight until the festival was over.

"Wow!" Benny exclaimed as they came into the square. "Look at all the people!"

A blue truck was parked next to the statue of Josiah Wade.

"The construction crew is here," Henry said.

"Yes, this is the crew Sylvia Pepper hired to build the booths," Jessie said.

"A lot of the booths are finished," Grandfather observed. "They must have gotten here early."

A few workers unloaded lumber by the town hall. Hammers rang out. Electric saws zipped through boards.

The statue of Josiah Wade was temporarily blocked from view. The workers had erected scaffolding around the statue and covered it with canvas to prevent damage.

A short man with scruffy hair carried a stepladder. When he saw the Aldens, he waved.

"That guy reminds me of our dog," Benny said. "His hair sticks out just like Watch's does."

"I'm going to see if the men have everything they need," said Grandfather.

"And we'll get to work," Henry said. The Aldens were on cleanup duty, but they were also going to hunt for clues.

The shop owners were busy, too. Ms. Reit and Sylvia Pepper were putting the finishing touches on their shop windows. Mr. Ames from the hardware store was hanging a large banner that proclaimed, GREENFIELD WINTER FESTIVAL.

"Look up there!" Benny cried. He pointed to a figure sitting on top of a lamppost. "It's Dawn!"

Dawn shinnied down the lamppost. She wore her camera around her neck.

"The things a photographer has to do to take good pictures!" Dawn said, joining the children.

"Weren't you scared up there?" Violet asked.

"I'm not crazy about heights, but that was the best place to get shots of the rooftops."

"I don't think I could climb a lamppost just to get a good picture," Violet said admiringly.

Dawn turned a small crank on her camera, rewinding the film. "Well, that's the last of this roll of film. I think I have enough shots for the souvenir booklet."

Jessie pulled a flier from her notebook. "Grandfather had stacks of these printed. People can order your booklet tomorrow at the festival."

"I'm taking souvenir pictures, too," Violet said to Dawn. "People will pay a dollar and I'll send them the picture later, after I have the film developed."

"Why don't you let me develop them for you?" Dawn said. "I can do it much cheaper than the lab the drugstore uses."

"That would be great!" Violet paused, then added nervously, "I've only taken pictures of the family. This is my first real assignment."

"You should take a few test shots," Dawn advised. "Pose a model by the statue today, just to see what the light is like. That way you'll know exactly where to stand to-morrow."

"I'll be your model, Violet," Benny volunteered.

Dawn patted Violet's arm. "You'll do just fine. Now I'd better get into my darkroom and develop this film."

Violet watched the young woman disappear into her studio. "I can't believe she's the phantom of Greenfield Square. She's just too nice."

"I know," Henry agreed. "But if Dawn was in the square last night, why didn't she say anything about seeing us? We can't rule out anyone as a suspect."

"Let's get started looking for clues," Jessie said. "Why don't we each take a corner of the square? We'll meet at the statue."

Henry nodded. "Good plan, Jessie. We

can always count on you to keep us organized."

Jessie blushed as she passed out small trash bags. "I'll take the corner by the town hall. Pick up trash and anything that looks suspicious."

Benny combed the ground near the parking lot. He found bottle caps and straw wrappers, which he threw into the garbage bag. But nothing else.

Too many people had walked around that morning, he concluded. Any clues the phantom had left behind would have been destroyed.

He had almost reached the statue when he saw something red between two bricks in the pavement.

A scrap of red silk.

He pulled it out. It was a ribbon, like the kind Dawn Wellington used around her ponytail.

"It's lunchtime!" Grandfather's voice boomed across the square.

Stuffing the ribbon in his pocket, Benny ran to Cooke's Drugstore.

"I never thought you'd be last to a meal!" Grandfather teased Benny as they all went inside.

They each chose a stool and ordered. Mrs. Turner assured them that apple pie with warm cinnamon sauce was on the menu.

Violet sat next to Benny. She had been taking practice pictures while she searched for clues in the square.

"I saw you pick something up," she said, putting her camera in her lap. "What did you find?"

Benny pulled the ribbon from his pocket. "This looks like Dawn's."

"It does," Violet agreed with a sinking heart. "But she could have lost it anytime." She was sure her special friend was not the phantom.

Sylvia Pepper came in while the Aldens were eating. She went over to Grandfather and said, "How do you like the construction crew I hired?"

"They seem to be just fine," James Alden replied. "Won't you join us for a bite to eat?"

"No, thanks," Sylvia replied. "I just wanted to see how things were going." Then she added, "I hope when the town votes to move the statue, you'll remember who helped you with this festival."

"A lot of people have helped," Grandfather said evenly. "But I do appreciate your efforts, Miss Pepper."

"The town won't want to move the statue anyway," Henry said when Sylvia had left. "I'm positive of that."

"We won't know until the votes are tallied," said Grandfather. "Rick Bass offered to help count the ballots tonight."

The young museum director also wanted the statue moved, thought Henry. He hadn't seen Rick that day and wondered where he was.

After lunch, they all went back outside. Two workmen were tying a tarpaulin over the blue truck bed. The stands and booths were finished. The scaffolding had been removed from the statue, but the canvas remained.

"That's our booth," Jessie said, checking a chart in her notebook. "It's right next to the refreshment booth."

"Yummy!" Benny liked the idea of being next to the cookie booth.

Violet took out her camera. "Benny, why don't you go over by the statue now? I want to check the light."

Benny ran over to the statue. As he leaned against the crumbling base, he wondered why the statue was still covered.

Lifting one corner, he peered under the cloth.

He couldn't believe his eyes.

The statue was gone!

CHAPTER 9

Vanished into Thin Air!

Violet was trying to focus through the viewfinder. But Benny kept moving the canvas that covered the statue.

"Look!" he cried. He grabbed a corner of the canvas and pulled.

Violet nearly dropped her camera. Standing on the granite base was a *stepladder*. The statue of Josiah Wade was missing!

Jessie clutched Henry's sleeve. "What happened to the statue?" she gasped.

"Someone took it!" Henry replied as they ran to the center of the square.

"Our statue's been kidnapped," Benny exclaimed, hopping with excitement. "I mean, statue-napped! Do you think the phantom of Greenfield Square did it?"

"There is no phantom," Henry told him. "But someone very clever pulled this off. We have to tell Grandfather."

James Alden was already on the scene. He stared at the stepladder in disbelief. "How in the world did someone steal a six-foot-high statue in broad daylight?"

Word of the theft buzzed around the square. Shop owners came out to stare at the ladder perched on the statue's base.

Rick Bass came running over. "This is incredible! Did anybody see anything?"

The Aldens shook their heads.

"People have been working in the square since this morning," said Grandfather. "That statue didn't vanish into thin air."

"The statue was covered all day," said Rick. "It could have been taken early this morning and we wouldn't have known the difference."

Violet thought of something. "Does this

mean the festival won't go on?"

Could they have a Winter Festival without the Minuteman statue? One of the main reasons for the event was to raise funds to fix the statue's base. Now the guest of honor was missing.

"The festival will go on as scheduled," Grandfather said firmly.

"The statue might turn up before tomorrow. It could be a prank," Rick said.

"Some prank!" Henry said. Was Rick Bass truly concerned or putting on an act?

"I'm going to talk to the shop owners," James Alden declared. "An operation like this couldn't be pulled off without somebody seeing *something*."

"I'll call the police," Rick offered. "They should be notified of the theft."

"Good idea," Grandfather said. He and Rick hurried off.

"The thief must have left clues," said Benny. "Let's look around."

The children searched the area thoroughly. But they found only bent nails and trash the construction workers had left behind.

Discouraged, Violet sat down on the statue's base. Her camera swung around her neck on its strap.

Jessie stared at the camera. "Violet!" she cried. "Your camera!"

"What about it?"

"You've been taking pictures all day. I bet you have a clue on your film!" Jessie said. How could they miss something so obvious?

Now Benny was excited. "If we develop the pictures, we might find out who stole the statue!"

"But the drugstore has to send film away to the lab," Henry said. "That takes almost a week."

"Dawn will develop my film," said Violet. "She could do it fast in her studio."

"Dawn is one of our suspects," Jessie reminded her. "Suppose she's the person we're after?"

"That's a chance we have to take," said Henry.

Benny was already running across the square. "Hurry up!" he called back.

Inside Dawn's studio, the red light glowed above the darkroom door.

"That means she's inside developing pictures," Violet said. She knocked on the door.

"Just a second," came the reply. A moment later, Dawn opened the door. She smiled when she saw the Aldens.

"Hi, what's up?"

The children told her the statue was missing and a valuable clue to the theft might be in Violet's pictures.

Dawn couldn't believe the statue of Josiah Wade was gone. She went to the window.

"It really is gone!" she said. "Let's develop Violet's film right away. You kids can help me."

They followed Dawn into her darkroom.

She put the roll of film into a canister of developing solution. Violet agitated the canister, then Dawn added other chemicals. Next, Dawn hung the roll of film up to dry. Jessie and Benny cut the negatives into strips.

"Now we print the pictures," Dawn said.

"But first we have to make the image bigger. I use this machine, called an enlarger."

She gave them prints as she enlarged the negatives.

The Aldens dipped the prints in trays of developing solution. Like magic, images appeared on the paper.

"Look at this!" Henry cried. With tweezers, he held up a photograph of the short, scruffy-haired worker talking to a woman.

The woman was Sylvia Pepper.

"Sylvia hired the construction crew," Violet said. "She must know the workers."

"Wait till you see this!" Jessie held up another picture.

The photograph showed the construction truck pulling away from the square. A tarpaulin covered the truck bed. Sticking out from the canvas was the end of a musket.

"Josiah's musket!" Benny exclaimed. "The workers stole the statue. We have to tell Grandfather!"

Violet was examining Jessie's photograph with a magnifying glass. "Look," she said. "Behind that pole. See anybody familiar?"

"Sylvia!" answered Benny, who had the sharpest eyes. "She's watching the truck leave."

"I think Miss Pepper has some explaining to do," Henry said decisively. "Let's go visit her."

Dawn shut off the equipment in her darkroom. "I'll come with you."

They went outside. All the shop owners were talking about the theft. Even the substitute pharmacist, Mr. Kirby, seemed concerned. Only Sylvia Pepper was absent.

She was in her shop, calmly putting a bouquet of yellow roses in water.

When she saw the Aldens, Sylvia said, "If it's about dressing up as a clown tomorrow for the festival, I've already told your grandfather I won't do it."

"But did you tell him about who stole the statue?" Jessie asked.

Sylvia dropped a rose. "What are you talking about?"

"Surely you must know the Minuteman statue is gone," Dawn said, gesturing toward the square. "It was stolen sometime today."

"Why would I know anything about it?" Sylvia said defensively. "I've been in my shop all day."

"Not the whole day." Henry put the two photographs on the counter.

Sylvia turned pale. Her bright lipstick seemed redder.

"Would you like to explain?" Dawn demanded.

The florist sat down on a stool behind the counter. "I thought I could get away with it," she said dully. "It was risky taking the statue in the middle of the day. But I believed we could pull it off."

"We, who?" Henry asked. "This man in the photo?"

"Yes," replied Sylvia. "His name is Don. We went to college together."

"Why did Don take the statue?" Benny asked. "It belongs to Greenfield."

Sylvia told them that years ago when she was in college, she saw a copy of Franklin Bond's sketch for the statue. She read the note about Josiah's gift to the sculptor.

"I never forgot about the secret compartment in the drawing," she explained. "I figured the gift — whatever it was — was hidden inside the statue."

Sylvia moved to Greenfield and opened her florist shop. But business was not as good as she'd hoped it would be and Sylvia was in danger of losing her lease on the store.

"Every day I'd look out on the square and see that statue," she said. "I knew it contained a secret."

"And you decided to take it," Henry concluded.

Sylvia nodded. "Josiah Wade lived during the Revolutionary War. Whatever he gave Franklin Bond would be very old and valuable. Collectors pay good money for any kind of Revolutionary relic."

"Like the things Rick Bass has in the museum," Violet said.

Sylvia went on. "I asked my old friend Don to help me look for the statue's secret. But I didn't want anybody to suspect me, so we arranged a private signal."

Benny slapped the counter. "The message photograph!"

"That's right," Sylvia said. "I learned that trick in a photography class. But then the photographs got all mixed up in the drugstore and I lost my message photo."

"I had it," Violet said. "And you figured it out. You took my camera that day."

Sylvia frowned. "It wasn't easy getting it back. I had to search all your belongings before I found it."

"What did the message mean?" Jessie said. " 'Move it the day before'?"

"The day before the festival," Sylvia said. "Since a lot of activity would be going on in the square, I thought that would be a good time to steal the statue."

"Why go to all that trouble?" Henry wanted to know. "Why not just call your friend and tell him about your plan?"

Sylvia shrugged. "I was afraid the call might be traced back to me."

"Then you didn't really mean it when you said the statue should be moved in front of your store," Benny accused.

Sylvia smiled. "I just said that."

"You're the phantom vandal," Violet said.

"You painted the statue and switched the building numbers. You even wrecked the decorations, didn't you?"

"I had to stall for time while I looked for the message photograph," Sylvia said. "Of course, I fired the original construction crew your grandfather hired. Don got a job as a construction worker and I hired his crew."

Jessie thought of something. "You made that call to Grandfather about moving the statue, didn't you?"

"Sure, to throw suspicion on Rick Bass. He never liked me, anyway," Sylvia said sourly. "Nobody likes me."

"We tried to," Dawn told her. "Everyone in the square would have pitched in to help save your shop."

"What do you care?" Sylvia said, tossing her head.

"The other night, after we worked on the wreaths," Dawn said. "You thought I had gone home, but I saw you poking around the statue."

"We saw you!" Henry cried. "We were

coming back for Jessie's notebook. You ran."

"I thought it was Sylvia coming back," Dawn said. "I didn't want her to think I was spying on her."

Sylvia gave a sharp laugh. "Well, let me tell you what I was doing. I was looking for the secret compartment one last time."

"The ribbon I found," Benny said. "It was yours, not Dawn's!" The scrap of cloth matched the bows on the door wreaths. Sylvia had contributed those ribbons.

Dawn looked at the Aldens in surprise. "Did you think I was the vandal?"

Violet blushed. "Well . . . we knew you were in the drugstore the day the pictures were mixed up."

"I was only in there a second," Dawn said. "The place was so crowded, I left."

"We couldn't rule out anyone," Henry told her, "until we got to the bottom of this. But we found the true culprit."

The corners of Sylvia's mouth turned down. "I really didn't want to steal that stupid statue."

A voice said behind them, "That's too bad, Miss Pepper. You could have saved us all a lot of trouble."

Violet turned at the voice. "Grandfather! Sylvia Pepper and her friend stole the statue!"

"I heard," James Alden said, striding into the shop. A policeman was at his heels. "You'll be happy to know, children, that the statue has been recovered."

CHAPTER 10

The Surprise in the Statue

Benny was the first to glimpse the flatbed truck.

"It's here!" he cried.

All the people who worked around the town square were on hand for the return of the stolen statue. Dawn Wellington and Mrs. Turner waited with the Aldens. Even Mr. Kirby came out for the event.

A cheer went up as the truck bumped over the curb and on into the square. Grandfather and Henry directed the truck to park next to the statue's granite block base.

Rick Bass hopped out of the passenger side of the truck. "We'll set the statue on the pavement," he told Grandfather. "We're going to fix Josiah's base eventually. But at least he's here for the festival."

"And just in time," Benny added. "The festival is tomorrow!"

Jessie hugged her notebook. So much had happened in the last few hours! Sylvia Pepper had confessed to stealing the Minuteman statue. Then the police took Miss Pepper away for questioning.

Rick Bass had spotted the statue when a policeman stopped Sylvia's accomplice after he'd run a red light. Rick had called for a truck to bring the statue to the square.

Now Josiah Wade was back in his rightful place.

Jessie watched as Mr. Kirby and Henry helped Rick and the driver unload the statue off the truck bed. She wondered if the town would vote to move the statue or keep it in the center of the square. The Alden children would find out later, when they helped Grandfather count the votes.

When the men were about to hoist the statue upright, Benny scooted forward.

"Can you tip it up?" he asked. "I want to look for something."

"Good thinking!" Rick said. "No better time to check for Franklin's surprise."

The driver braced his end of the statue. "We can hold it for a few seconds."

Benny knelt down. The statue was hollow inside, like a giant chocolate bunny. Grandfather handed him a small flashlight. Benny shined the light inside the statue.

"See anything?" Violet asked.

"No," Benny replied, disappointed.

"Oh, well," Rick said consolingly. "We were never really certain Franklin Bond put his gift inside the statue. We were just guessing."

"Franklin Bond liked to play jokes," Henry said. "Maybe he just pretended to put a secret compartment in the statue."

But Benny had been so sure. The statue was the perfect place to hide something.

The men lowered the statue and stood it

upright beside the granite base. Grandfather gave the driver a generous tip before he drove the truck out of the town square.

"Now the square looks normal again." Dawn sighed. "It just wasn't the same without Josiah standing there."

"Let's hope Greenfield feels the same way you do," said Grandfather. "I have the ballot box in my car. Why don't you and Rick come home with us and help count votes?"

"Great idea!" Violet said. She was so glad Dawn hadn't turned out to be the Greenfield phantom.

Rick glanced at Dawn. "I'd like to, but we hate to impose."

"Mrs. McGregor loves company," Jessie assured them.

The Aldens got into Grandfather's car. Rick and Dawn followed in Rick's battered station wagon.

The housekeeper was delighted to set two extra places at the dining room table. "It's pot roast night," said Mrs. McGregor to the guests. "There's more than enough."

While they ate pot roast, mashed potatoes,

and carrots, they discussed Sylvia Pepper's theft.

"I don't see how she thought she could get away with it," said Dawn. "What was she going to do with the statue after she stole it?"

"She probably never thought that far ahead," said Grandfather. "People behave strangely when they need money."

"I guess she was desperate to keep her shop," Rick added, helping himself to another biscuit. "The florist shop will close now, for sure."

Jessie passed Rick the butter. "Do you think Franklin Bond really put a secret compartment in his statue?"

"It sure seemed that way on the drawing," Rick allowed. "I guess Franklin changed his mind. Maybe he lost Josiah's gift or sold it."

Benny admired the young man's appetite. Rick had eaten five biscuits, breaking Benny's record of four!

After dinner, they gathered in the living room to count the ballots. Grandfather built a cozy fire. Mrs. McGregor brought in a tray of hot chocolate.

"I'll help, too," the housekeeper offered. "Many hands make light work, as my mother used to say."

Benny emptied the ballot box on the floor. They all grabbed handfuls of ballots.

"We'll make two piles," said Grandfather. "One pile of votes to keep the statue in the square. And the other for votes to move it."

With eight of them sorting ballots, the work went quickly.

When Grandfather tallied the last vote, he smiled. "The town voted by a wide margin to keep the statue in the square!"

"Yay!" Benny tossed ballots into the air like confetti.

Jessie giggled at her brother, then began picking up the slips of paper.

Violet remembered that Rick wanted the statue in his museum. "I hope you don't feel bad," she said to him.

"I'm glad," Rick said. "Dawn's right. Greenfield wouldn't be Greenfield without Josiah in the square."

"All of our problems are solved," said Grandfather. "Except one."

Jessie knew what he meant. "We still need a clown."

Dawn grinned at Rick. "I bet that suit will fit you!"

"I've always wanted to wear a rubber nose," Rick said. "We'd better go. Clowns need lots of beauty sleep."

Grandfather showed them to the door. "See you at the festival!"

When their guests had left, the Alden children went upstairs to get ready for bed.

Benny dragged his fingers slowly along the handrail. He was glad the statue would stay in the square where it belonged. But he wondered about Franklin Bond's secret compartment.

Did the sculptor have the last laugh on Greenfield after all?

"Smile!" Violet adjusted the focus on her camera, then snapped the picture.

The young father and his two children stepped away from the statue.

"Next!" called Benny. A couple of teenagers posed by Josiah Wade. Benny made sure they stood in the right spot, then signaled to Violet.

Crowds jammed the square. People had driven in from neighboring towns to buy cookies and pies from the bakery booth, play games, and listen to the high school marching band.

The Aldens' souvenir photo booth was very busy. Henry collected the fee. Jessie filled out the order forms, so they would know where to send each photo after it was developed. Benny positioned people next to the statue, and Violet took the pictures.

Benny was glad they were busy. But he wished he had time to play one of the games. He wanted to win a prize.

Grandfather had already given his speech and announced the results of the vote. Everyone seemed happy that the statue would remain in the square.

Dawn ran up. "Mr. Kirby is watching my booth for a second. I just wanted to tell you that I've sold over seventy souvenir booklets!"

"That's great!" Jessie said. "Violet's sold a lot of pictures, too."

Grandfather strolled over to the children's booth. "Thanks to your help, the festival is a great success. We should have plenty of money to fix Josiah's base."

"So he can rule Greenfield Square for many more years," Henry added.

Just then Rick Bass bounded over. All morning, he had danced around the square in the purple and green clown suit, entertaining little children.

"My feet are killing me," he said, tugging off one of his huge, floppy clown shoes and handing it to Jessie.

Jessie laughed. With his big round nose and orange hair, Rick made a terrific clown.

"Will you take my picture?" Rick teased Violet. "How do I look?" He performed a wobbly handstand in front of Josiah Wade's statue.

Violet was giggling so hard, she could barely push the shutter. "This will be a terrific picture!"

"Watch out!" Benny cried, just as Rick's legs toppled over.

Rick had landed upside down against the granite base of the statue. Henry and Jessie ran over and helped him up.

"Ow." Rick winced. "Uh-oh. Looks like I knocked off a few more stones."

"It's okay," James Alden reassured him. "Just as long as you aren't hurt."

Benny was staring at a hole just beneath the brass plaque. Rick's fall had caused the stones to cave in, revealing a dark space.

"Hey!" he cried. "The statue has a secret after all!"

Rick gave a long, low whistle. "What do you know? We never thought of looking in the *base*! Benny, since you found it, you should do the honors."

With everyone watching intently, Benny reached into the compartment. His fingers closed around a small metal box.

"Should I open it?" he asked.

Grandfather nodded.

Holding his breath, Benny unlatched the

box and lifted the lid. Inside was a ball of wrinkled yellow paper.

"That's parchment," Rick said. "It's very old."

Benny unfolded the paper. A small object rolled into his palm.

"A button," he said, puzzled. "Franklin Bond put a *button* in his secret compartment?"

"Let me see that." Rick rubbed the button on the sleeve of his clown costume. Black streaks marked the purple satin. "It's genuine silver."

"There's something engraved on it," Jessie said. " 'G. W.' "

"I wonder what that could stand for," Violet said.

But Henry knew. He had read about the Revolutionary War. "George Washington!" he exclaimed.

"Good guess!" Rick said. "General George Washington was head of the Colonial army."

Dawn frowned. "But why would the

sculptor hide one of George Washington's buttons inside the base of his statue?"

"We know that Josiah Wade carried secret messages in his jacket buttons during the war," Rick said. "Maybe General Washington gave Josiah one of his own buttons. Maybe as a reward."

"And Josiah gave the button to Franklin Bond," Jessie concluded. "Who hid it in the base of his statue of Josiah Wade. It all makes sense!"

Grandfather inspected the button. "This will be a nice addition to the Greenfield museum."

"A new artifact!" Benny declared.

He was thrilled he had discovered the statue's secret. That was better than a prize any day.

Violet was happy, too. The Winter Festival was a success and the Aldens had solved another mystery.

"Smile!" she said, snapping a photo of the Alden family. She knew the picture would turn out just great.

GERTRUDE CHANDLER WARNER discovered when she was teaching that many readers who like an exciting story could find no books that were both easy and fun to read. She decided to try to meet this need, and her first book, *The Boxcar Children*, quickly proved she had succeeded.

Miss Warner drew on her own experiences to write the mystery. As a child she spent hours watching trains go by on the tracks opposite her family home. She often dreamed about what it would be like to set up housekeeping in a caboose or freight car — the situation the Alden children find themselves in.

When Miss Warner received requests for more adventures involving Henry, Jessie, Violet, and Benny Alden, she began additional stories. In each, she chose a special setting and introduced unusual or eccentric characters who liked the unpredictable.

While the mystery element is central to each of Miss Warner's books, she never thought of them as strictly juvenile mysteries. She liked to stress the Aldens' independence and resourcefulness and their solid New England devotion to using up and making do. The Aldens go about most of their adventures with as little adult supervision as possible — something else that delights young readers.

Miss Warner lived in Putnam, Connecticut, until her death in 1979. During her lifetime, she received hundreds of letters from girls and boys telling her how much they liked her books.